FARM LIFE LONG AGO

Written by Tim Johnson

STECK-VAUGHN
ELEMENTARY · SECONDARY · ADULT · LIBRARY

A Harcourt Classroom Education Company

www.steck-vaughn.com

Long ago, living on a farm was hard work.
Families worked together to farm the land.
They raised crops to eat and sell.
They raised animals to help with farm
work and also for food.

Everyone in the family helped out.
They got up very early each morning.
Everyone had much work to do.
They gathered eggs, milked cows, and
fed the animals.

In spring, farmers planted their crops.
Often farmers planted one kind of seed.
Horses pulled plows through the fields.
Then farmers planted their seeds.

Farmers planted their crops in rows.
First they placed the seeds in the ground.
Next they covered the seeds with soil.
Then farmers waited for rain to make the
seeds begin to grow.

Most baby animals were born in the spring.
Children on the farm often cared for them.
They fed the baby animals every day.
Children also kept them safe from danger.

In summer, farmers had much work to do.
It was often very hot and dry.
They had to be sure plants got water.
Many farmers built windmills to pull water
up from the ground.

After a hot day of work, farmers rested.
They looked for a cool, shady place.
Some farmers told stories of days gone by.
Children gathered around and listened to
the wonderful tales.

Later in summer, some crops were ripe.
Everyone worked hard to pick them.
Horses pulled wagons beside the fields.
Farmers put all they had harvested into
the wagons.

In fall, farmers harvested the last crops.
Some crops were canned or dried.
They were stored for the winter.
The rest of the crops were taken to
town and sold.

Many towns held a farmer's market.
Nearby farmers sold the harvest there.
They bought seeds with their money.
They also bought clothes and shoes
for their families.

Children began school in the fall.
They usually went to a one-room school.
Children of all ages were in one class.
They learned reading, writing, and math.

Then farmers got ready for the winter.
They plowed the fields again.
They fixed broken fences.
Farmers also chopped wood to use for
heating and cooking.

During winter, farmers fixed their
wagons and plows.
They put extra hay in the barns.
They gathered the animals together.
Farmers gave them plenty to eat.

In winter, families usually stayed inside.
Children learned to cook or build things.
Families ate canned and dried foods.
Hot food kept everyone warm.

Long ago, living on a farm was hard work.
Everyone in the family had to help.
Today farmers use machines to help.
But farming is still very hard work.